W9-ADR-420

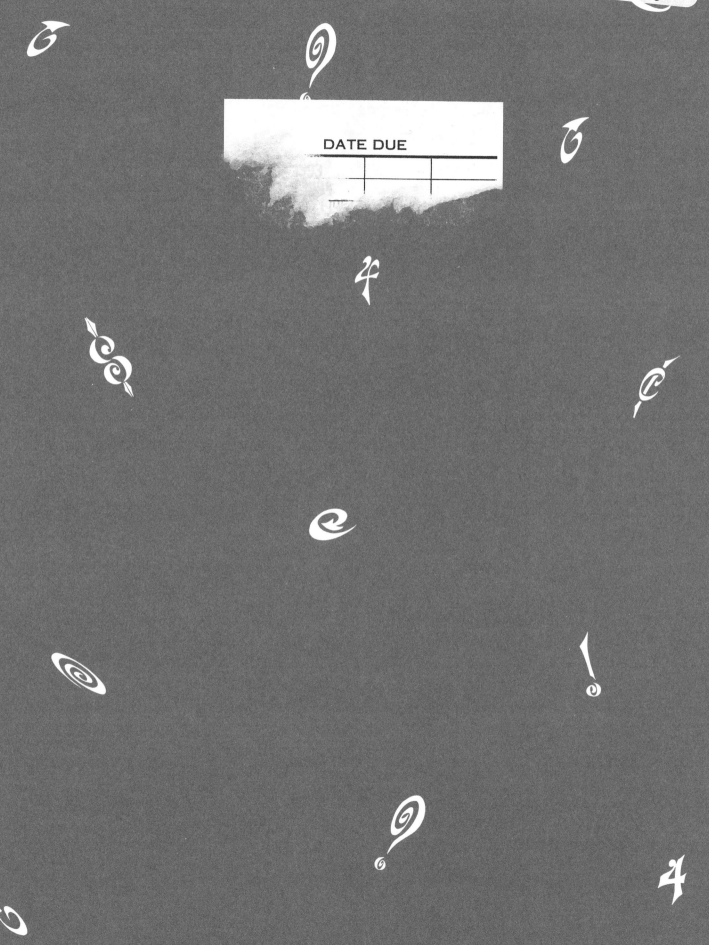

DATE DUE

# ALICE

# WHOOPI GOLDBERG

Illustrations by John Rocco

**BANTAM BOOKS**
New York  Toronto  London  Sydney  Auckland

ALICE

A Bantam Book / October 1992

*BOOK DESIGN BY CAROL MALCOLM-RUSSO*

Library of Congress Number: 92-15935
ISBN 0-553-08990-0

Published simultaneously in the United States and Canada

Bantam Books are published by Bantam Books, a division of Bantam
Doubleday Dell Publishing Group, Inc. Its trademark, consisting of the
words "Bantam Books" and the portrayal of a rooster, is Registered in
U.S. Patent and Trademark Office and in other countries. Marca
Registrada. Bantam Books, 666 Fifth Avenue, New York, New York 10103.

PRINTED IN THE UNITED STATES OF AMERICA

KPP    0 9 8 7 6 5 4 3 2 1

To my mother,
Alex and Amarah,
Maurice Sendak,
Steven Spielberg,
Mike Nichols,
"T,"
and to everyone
who has ever had a dream

**W**hen she woke up that morning, Alice knew things were going to be different.

It wasn't anything she could put her finger on, exactly. She still lived in New Jersey with her mother and father. Her best friend was still a sort of invisible rabbit from Italy (so he said) who sounded a lot like that actor Robert De Niro and called himself Salvador De Rabbit. Alice called him Sal. Robin, who was her best visible friend, still lived next door.

The other thing that hadn't changed was that Alice wanted, more than anything in the world, to be rich. She wanted big cars, diamonds, butlers with funny jackets, maids to cater to her every wish, and exciting, fun adventures—everything that money could buy. Not that her life was so bad. But if she were rich, she thought, then she'd really know what it meant to be happy.

That's why Alice made a habit of entering every sweepstakes, every giveaway, every contest in the world. Didn't matter where it was, didn't matter what it was for. If something said "send me in," she did. Everyone told her she'd never win, that it was all a pipe dream.

They'd say, "Alice, money isn't everything." But she'd just smile and think, It is for me; when you're rich, you can have anything you want.

Well, so far, she'd never won a thing. Day after day she'd look into her mailbox, just waiting for that fat envelope to appear. Day after day it was empty. But you know how it is—sometimes you just get a feeling, and sure enough . . . BLAM! Something hits you. That's what happened to Alice.

$S$al was waiting for Alice after school as usual that day. They had agreed long ago not to talk until they were where no one could see them. Alice was considered a little odd anyway; no need to give people any more to talk about. When they got closer to home and her mailbox was in sight, Alice said, "Sal, I think today is the day."

"Oh yeah? Why's that?"

"I don't know, I just have a feeling."

Robin was sitting on his stoop waiting for them. Most people thought Robin was a little bit weird, too. He wore a funny top hat and an oversized coat, and he was always trying to figure out card tricks that he never could get right. He didn't care what other people said. He liked his coat and his hat and his tricks. Besides, for as long as they could remember,

Robin was the only other person who could see and speak to Sal. So the three of them together, well, they were quite a team.

"Say hey hey."

"Hey, Robin."

"What's up?"

"Well," began Sal, "Alice here thinks today's her lucky day."

"Again?"

"Yes," Alice replied, a little annoyed, "again."

"Okay, let's open her up," Robin said. Everyone took a deep breath. They'd been through this before, and both Robin and Sal had a hard time seeing Alice disappointed. They all promised to stick together, though, no matter what.

Alice opened the mailbox door. Sure enough, there was an envelope inside. Her hands began to sweat as she slowly pulled it toward her. "Something's here . . . please let it be something good."

Now Robin began to sweat. His coat felt ten times heavier than it had the minute before. "Come on, hurry up, I'm starting to sweat, too," Sal said. Sal liked to say he was a man trapped in a rabbit

suit, and Alice and Robin would have to remind him that he was just a semi-invisible rabbit and fur was part of the deal.

"Don't start with that again, Sal," Alice pleaded. "This is serious . . . I'm scared."

"Hey, don't be. What's the worst that could happen?"

"You're right." And feeling a little braver, Alice pulled the envelope all the way out of the box. Her name was right there on the front in big red writing.

"Well?" Sal whispered. "Gonna open it or what?"

"Oh, be still, Sal," Alice cried. She slid her thumb under the back flap and slipped it open. What if . . . What if . . .

Alice pulled out the letter and unfolded it slowly, carefully, as if it were a time bomb ready to explode. Her hands were shaking. She wondered if Robin and Sal could hear the pounding of her heart.

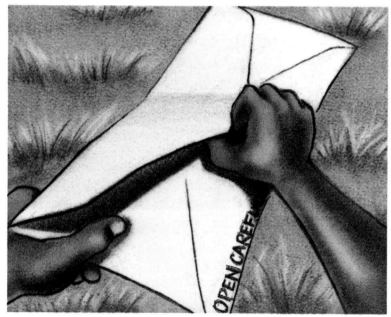

"You read it, Robin," she said, covering her eyes and shoving it at him.

"Not me, I can hardly breathe."

"Sal?"

"Forget it, kid. This one's all yours."

Finally, Alice looked down at the page.

DEAR WINNER, it said.

Alice read it again.

DEAR WINNER, it still said.

"Oh, oh, oh," she gasped.

"What?" the others asked.

"Oh, oh, oh" was all she could say.

"What?" Robin screamed.

"Oh."

"Oh, oh, oh, yeah, yeah, yeah. Just let me see this," Sal said, taking charge the way he often would.

" 'Dear Winner," Sal read,

" 'Congrats on winning first prize in the Wegonnagetcha Sweepstakes. Your prize worth big bucks awaits you at 4444 Forty-fourth Street, New York, ground floor. And congrats again.

Signed,
The Wedungotcha Corp.' "

"I—I won! I won! I won!" Alice chanted. She knew today was the day. Hadn't she said it? Hadn't she known? From now on, it would be limos and servants and anything she wanted. Isn't it great? Isn't it grand? All she could do was cha-cha.

Needless to say, even Sal was excited, in his cool way. Robin was so ecstatic, he gave Alice a big hug, practically lifting her off the ground. He had never seen her so happy.

"So what are you going to do, Alice?"

"What do you mean? Why, we're going to collect that prize."

"Well, um, where is New York, anyway?" Robin asked cautiously.

"Across the river."

"Ever been there before?" Sal wanted to know.

"Well, no," said Alice.

"Know how to get there?"

"Actually, no."

"So I repeat, Alice, what are you gonna do?"

She hated when Sal made sense, which he always did, but here was a question that needed answering. "Okay, first we'll get on a bus to New York. Then we'll get ourselves a map and find this 4444 Forty-fourth Street."

"How do we pay for the bus?" Sal asked. Sense again, right again.

"Well, I've got some birthday money upstairs," Alice said.

"I've been saving my allowance to get a computer," Robin added, "but if it will get us to New York, let's use it!"

"I'll buy that computer for you, Robin." He knew Alice would because that's the kind of girl she was. "Now that I'm rich, it's easy."

"Thanks, Alice, but I'd share it with you even if you weren't rich."

Alice was so lost in her world of fame and fortune that she missed that last part. "Meet you in two minutes," she said, running off into her house.

She knew she should tell someone where she was going, but she thought, When they all find out I'm rich, how could they be mad? So she smashed her bank, gathered her money, and ran out to meet up with the others. It was a short walk to the bus stop, and after waiting impatiently they boarded the big, silver bus. Sal didn't need to buy a ticket (you know how it is with invisible rabbits—they pretty much ride free).

On the bus they all watched out their windows as the buildings of the New York skyline got bigger the closer they got to the city. None of them had ever been there except for Sal, who had visited once as a bunny (so he said). They were all so excited, they could barely stay in their seats.

Soon they pulled out of a tunnel and into the streets of the city. The buildings were so tall they seemed to bend over their heads. People raced up and down the blocks. Taxis filled the streets.

Feeling a little over-whelmed and a little hungry, Alice and her friends decided to stop off at a diner they'd seen on the way in. It was one of those old places with red vinyl booths, big checked linoleum floors, and shiny stools at the counter. Two identical waiters were taking orders and clearing up dirty dishes. Alice, Robin, and Sal slid onto stools at the counter and picked up menus.

"What'll it be?" asked one of the twins.

"Yeah, what'll it be?" asked the other twin.

"Hamburger," said Alice.

"Hamburger," said Robin.

"Hamburger," said Sal. No one heard that last one, Sal being invisible and all.

"Two succulent hamburgers," said one of the twins.

"Two scrumptious hamburgers," said the other.

"Um, make that two for me," Robin called out.

"Thanks," Sal mumbled, a little miffed at almost missing out on lunch. A cool thing, not to be seen, but sometimes Sal felt a little ignored.

"And two Cokes," said Robin.

"Orange soda, please," added Alice.

"Three succulent hamburgers, two sparkling Cokes, one slippery orange soda sliding simultaneously to your stomachs at supersonic speed," the twins hollered out in unison. They were off like a shot. They'd been doing this for a long time.

"Boy, it's noisy in here," Robin said, closing up his menu.

"We won't be here long. We've got to get that sweepstakes prize," said Alice. Suddenly, as if someone had turned off the sound, the room got very still. And before they could say another word, one of the twins had reappeared, leaning over them again, looking awfully interested. "You have a sweepstakes ticket that's a winner?"

"Yes, we're going to claim the prize," said Alice, a little taken aback. Suddenly the other twin was poking his head into the conversation. "What sort of prize?" he added.

"Don't know," Alice answered, "but it's worth big bucks."

The twins then started to speak so low and so fast that everyone had to lean in to understand them: "What a surprise! How sudden! What will you do with it? We think it's superb! May we supply our assistance? We're more than happy to supervise!"

It was Sal who noticed that all eyes in the room were now on them. It started to get very warm, steamy almost, and the colors got very bright and all three of them started to feel funny as if . . . well, it seemed that as those twins continued to chatter, the room began to shrink! The walls seemed to close in around them, shaking like jelly, the checks on the floor jumping up and slapping back down.

"Shall we pick up the prize for you? We're off work in just a little while, and we'd be more than happy to help you with it. We've never won anything, you know. Please, we're quite serious about our suggestions!"

It was Sal who noticed that all the other customers had surrounded them. Everyone in the room was getting louder and louder and louder, their faces getting bigger and stretchier. And as the room got smaller, the people leaned in closer, all of them saying the same thing: "She's a winner! She's a winner! She's a sweepstakes winner!"

Alice and Robin and Sal all had the same thought: Get out before this place gets any smaller. So, as fast as they could, they were history, leaving some money on the table and barely making it through the tiny front door. Once across the street, they watched as the diner got smaller and smaller, until it was the size of a Roach Motel. One by one, the customers popped back to normal size as they squeezed out into the street.

"Let's split," Alice said, feeling shaken up but pretty much normal size again. She couldn't get over how those people had acted. It's not my fault they aren't winners like me, she thought. I just got lucky.

"We'll see how lucky," Sal said. Sometimes he could hear people thinking.

"Sal!" Alice said.

"Sorry, kid. Hey, cheer up. We're going to collect your prize."

"Straight up," Robin said. And all three of them were ready to find a map and get on with their journey.

ow Alice assumed that Robin could read a map, and Robin assumed that Alice could read a map. Truth was, neither Robin nor Alice could, so when they actually found one, they were pretty stumped. That is, until Sal, as usual, solved their problem.

"The subway," he said to Alice. "The subway," she said to Robin. And they were off, down the stairs into the subway station, through the turnstile, and into a waiting car.

There's something about being on a train in New York that's like nothing else in the world. When the train is moving fast, the graffiti on other trains looks like the colors inside a kaleidoscope. There are all kinds of people, too, some reading, some staring into space, some staring at you. I could write a book about it but I won't because I'll bet you're wondering about Alice.

hey'd been on the train for some time when Sal announced, "This is our stop." And the three jumped off, the doors sliding shut behind them.

"Where are we?" Alice asked.

"We're here," Sal said.

"Where's *here*?" Alice wondered aloud, her voice echoing down the tunnel.

"Well, we're at ..." He looked at the wall, which had PARK AVENUE painted on it. "Park Avenue. Yeah, Park Avenue."

"Well, let's go," Alice said, tugging them up the stairs, "4444 Forty-fourth Street can't be all that far. How big could this city be, anyway?"

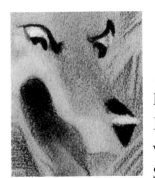It seemed they walked for hours looking for 4444 Forty-fourth Street. Alice's feet hurt and Robin was feeling especially sweaty in his coat. It hadn't occurred to them to read a street sign, which will generally tell you where you are. And Sal, who knew better, decided he'd let Alice figure this one out herself.

So, without giving much thought to the matter, Alice stopped a very large woman with very large everything: large fur, large face, large pearls, huge diamonds. I mean, she was big. Except for a tiny tiara she wore on her large hair.

There were other women walking with her who were large but not *as* large. Kind of a *smaller* large, if you catch my drift. Alice walked up to the largest woman and asked, "Excuse me, but can you tell me how to get to 4444 Forty-fourth Street?" The woman looked down at Alice as though she were a fly that had landed on her fur.

"Excuse me?"

Alice stepped back. She realized her question must have been blocked by the woman's very large bosom. "4444 Forty-fourth Street—can you tell me where it is, please?"

"Why?"

"Because . . ."

"Why, why, why," the large woman interrupted, "would anyone want to go to Forty-fourth Street?" She looked horrified. "Forty-fourth Street is . . . *downtown.*" The other ladies were also horrified—close to fainting, one of them.

"Downtown! Can you imagine?" one said.

"How could it be?" screeched the other.

"Who *is* this girl?" said the first.

Alice was a little annoyed by this treatment, as was Sal, though they couldn't see his annoyance, of course. Robin, whose mismatched ensemble drew horrified looks from the women, straightened his coat defiantly.

"My name is Alice, who are you?"

"Why, I am Mrs. Tu Lowdown, of course."

"Well, Mrs. Lowdown, what's wrong with downtown?" Alice asked.

"What's WRONG with … Well, young lady, I must tell you …
*We are the very, very rich
and our voices we pitch
high up and away
from the ground.
We rrrroll our rrrrr's
and stay very, very far
from all the ugly sounds.
From bookshops and fruit stops,
eyeglass wear and punklike hair,
we never, ever go downtown.*"

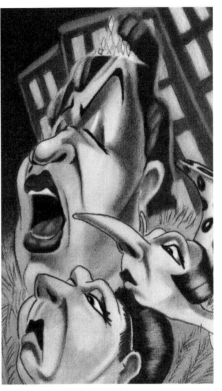

And with that, Mrs. Lowdown and her companions huffed away like a mother hen followed by her chicks. That is, all but one, who poked her long, pointy nose over her fur at Alice and whispered, "Why *are* you going downtown?"

"Because I have a sweepstakes ticket that's worth big bucks and—"

Before Alice could finish her sentence, Mrs. Lowdown was towering over her again.

"Big bucks, you say? How big?"

"Big," Robin said.

A smile crept over Mrs. Lowdown's large face. "Rrrrrrreally? Well, my dear, do come have some tea," she cooed, pulling Alice away from Sal and Robin. "Leave the boy with the atrocious outfit," she hissed in Alice's ear, "he's … well, he's not one of us. Big bucks, you say?"

**S**o this is what the life of the rich is like, Alice thought, as the women whisked her into a fancy building with a red-suited doorman out front. Robin and Sal were close behind, but when the doorman slammed the cast-iron gates shut with a clang, they had no choice but to wait.

What a house this Mrs. Lowdown had. Glaring chandeliers, oily paintings, big, squishy chairs. Soon, Alice thought, I'll be living in a place like this.

"Now let's just see this winning ticket, my dear," Mrs. Lowdown said to Alice. "So often they are falsified, and I'd be delighted to check if it's real." Something didn't seem right. Why did Mrs. Lowdown want to see the ticket? Besides, Alice wasn't feeling so good about leaving Sal and Robin outside.

"I can't stay long, my friends are waiting," Alice said weakly, as the pointy-nosed woman ran over and shoved a cup of tea in front of her.

"We're your friends now, darling. Besides, you really shouldn't be seen with that boy who dresses so horribly—what will people say? Now, sweetheart, just hand over that ticket."

"Well . . ." Alice hesitated.

"Do it now!" Mrs. Lowdown bellowed, her face growing red as if she were going to pop. It took everything in Alice's power to tear herself free from the chair, which seemed to be swallowing her up. "Stop her," Mrs. Lowdown screamed, but Alice was already running out the door, down the stairs, and past the doorman, where she stumbled over Sal and Robin.

"Let's get out of here," she cried, and they took off down the street.

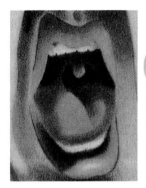**M**rs. Lowdown was, of course, beside herself with rage. After sending the ladies away, she called for her butler, Harry. "How dare she?" she wailed at him. "When I'm through with her, she'll wish she had never received that winning ticket! Get on the phone to Mr. Lowdown at *Lowdown News*. Tell him he must do everything in his power to find this Alice, the sweepstakes winner. She's out there and I want her stopped!"

"But, madam," her butler quivered, "you have everything you could ever want."

"A girl can *never* have enough money!" she snarled. "I want that ticket and I want it NOW!"

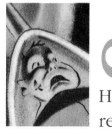 r. Lowdown knew better than to go against Mrs. Lowdown's wishes. So when he got Harry's call, he stopped the presses and put an artist's rendering of Alice on the front page of the evening edition. Mr. Lowdown sent his men out in airplanes to circle the entire city. He sent other men in cars, prowling the streets in search of Alice.

Who, meanwhile, hadn't stopped running yet.

"I've got to stop," Robin puffed.

"Not just yet, a little farther. We've got to get my prize before Mrs. Lowdown catches up with us."

"I can't," he said, and stopped, still huffing and puffing. "I have to stop."

And so they did.

"Hey!" yelled Sal.

"What?"

"Look over there." On the wall was a sign that read FORTUNE TELLER.

"Maybe the fortune teller can tell us where we can find 4444 Forty-fourth Street," Alice said hopefully, though at this point she wasn't so sure about anything. After knocking and not getting any answer, they opened the door themselves. They smelled all kinds of strange smells and saw all kinds of strange drawings of hands on the walls. "Hello?" Alice whispered.

"What do you want?"

Behind them appeared a woman with a scarf around her head, a bright dress, and lots of bangles. "Oh, you scared us!" Alice said, trying to catch her breath.

"Part of the job," the woman replied. "Well, what will it be? Palm read? Tea leaves? Rabbit food?"

"Rabbit food?" Alice asked.

"Yeah, for your friend there."

"You can see him?" asked Robin.

"Didn't I just point him out?"

"Wow," said Alice. "How—"

"Don't ask. I bet you want to discover what's in your future," the woman continued, closing her eyes and rolling her hand over her crystal ball. "I see . . . I see . . . I see nothing! Have you been messing with this ball?" She started smacking it, trying to get it going.

"We're looking for 4444 Forty-fourth Street," Alice interrupted.

"Oh," the woman sighed, "you have a winning ticket worth big bucks, right?"

"You're right!" Alice shouted. "How did you know?"

"Don't ask," the fortune teller said again, this time with sadness in her voice.

"I'm going to be rich and famous and have everything I ever wanted: big house, fun times, and lots of good friends—everything money can buy," Alice said.

"And you think money buys all that?" the woman asked, folding her arms across her chest.

"Of course," said Alice. "When you're rich, you can have whatever you want and do whatever you want."

"Well, go to it," said the woman, pointing to the door. "The place you're looking for is right across the street."

"Oh, we're here!" Alice cried, running out the door and leaving Robin and Sal behind.

"Let her go, she'll be right back," the woman said.

"How do you know?" said Robin. "Oh, I know—don't ask."

**B**efore long, Alice did come back. Her eyes were puffy with tears.

"What happened? Are you rich? What's wrong?" Robin and Sal couldn't stop asking questions. The fortune teller took Alice by the hand and sat her down. Alice was quiet for a few minutes.

"Well," asked Sal, "tell us what—"

"It was all a lie! There was just this weird lady sitting at a desk, filing her nails. My prize wasn't a prize at all. They just tricked me into coming in so they could sell me some swampland in Florida."

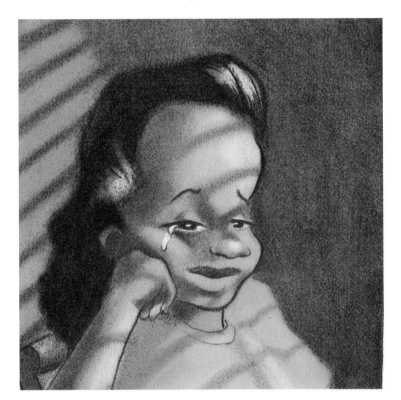

"What?"

"They wanted me to give *them* money. Since I wouldn't, they said I could have an electric can opener as a consolation prize . . . for $29.95."

"Some consolation," the fortune teller said.

"So there were no big bucks?" asked Sal.

"No."

"No prize?" asked Robin.

"No."

The room was very quiet until Alice finally spoke again. "I thought I was going to be rich and have everything I ever wanted."

The woman bent over to Alice and quietly said, "Dear, you *are* rich. Look at your wonderful friends who stick by you whether you win or lose. Think about the wild adventure you've had. No amount of money could buy those things."

Slowly, Alice began to understand. Everything she really wanted had been with her the whole time. Robin came over and gave her a hug. So did Sal.

"I'm sorry, you guys. You must think I'm awful," she said, looking at them in a whole different way.

"You're not awful," said Robin, "you're Alice." They all laughed.

"Now, come on, let's go home," Sal said.

"Good-bye, and thanks," Alice said to the woman as they walked out the door.

"No problem, and hey—send your friends. I'll get this ball working again."

As they filed out the door, Sal hesitated. "You go on ahead," he told the others. "I'll catch up." When he stepped back in the door, the fortune teller turned around.

"Thanks, Mom," he said, kissing her on the cheek.

"Let me get this thing off and I'll give you one right back." As the fortune teller unwrapped her scarf, her face began to change, revealing the head of a beautiful white rabbit, just like Sal.

"You keep taking good care of Alice, my sweetheart. I sent you to her for a reason: One day she'll be quite something. Thanks to you, she's already on her way."

"On her way to what? Oh, I know, I know—don't ask."

"Remember, her future is bright . . ." she called after him. And on that note, Sal ran to catch up with the others.

As they waited at the corner for the light to change, a giant roadster pulled up in front of them, coughing up gray smoke. And guess who poked her large, nasty face out of the window? Mrs. Tu Lowdown herself. Before Alice could react, six more cars pulled up, surrounding them on all sides.

"Why, Alice, what a perfectly delightful surprise. I've been looking all over for you! Do you still happen to have, by any chance, that silly old sweepstakes ticket?"

Robin looked at Sal. Sal looked at Alice. And feeling braver and more sure than ever, Alice looked Mrs. Lowdown straight in the eye and pulled out her ticket. She said, "Mrs. Lowdown, I'm happy to present you with this winning sweepstakes ticket worth big bucks. You deserve it."

"M e? Why, you shouldn't have!" Mrs. Lowdown said, snatching the ticket from Alice's hand, and without a moment's hesitation she growled, "Harry—to the claims office!"

As they walked up the block, Alice, Sal, and Robin heard yelling that was so loud, they couldn't quite understand the words. But those who were farther away pretty much agreed it sounded something like this:

"SWAMPLAND???"

 hen they finally made it home, Alice walked up and down her block. It was a nice one, and her house was nice, too. She looked at her two friends and thought, These are the best friends I could ever have. Suddenly, she felt a party coming on.

"Darlings," she said in her Lowdownest voice, "do come have some tea."

They all agreed it was an excellent idea.

And a fine time was had by all.

**P.S.** When Alice grew up, she became a foremost doctor of rabbitology.

At least that's the way I heard it.

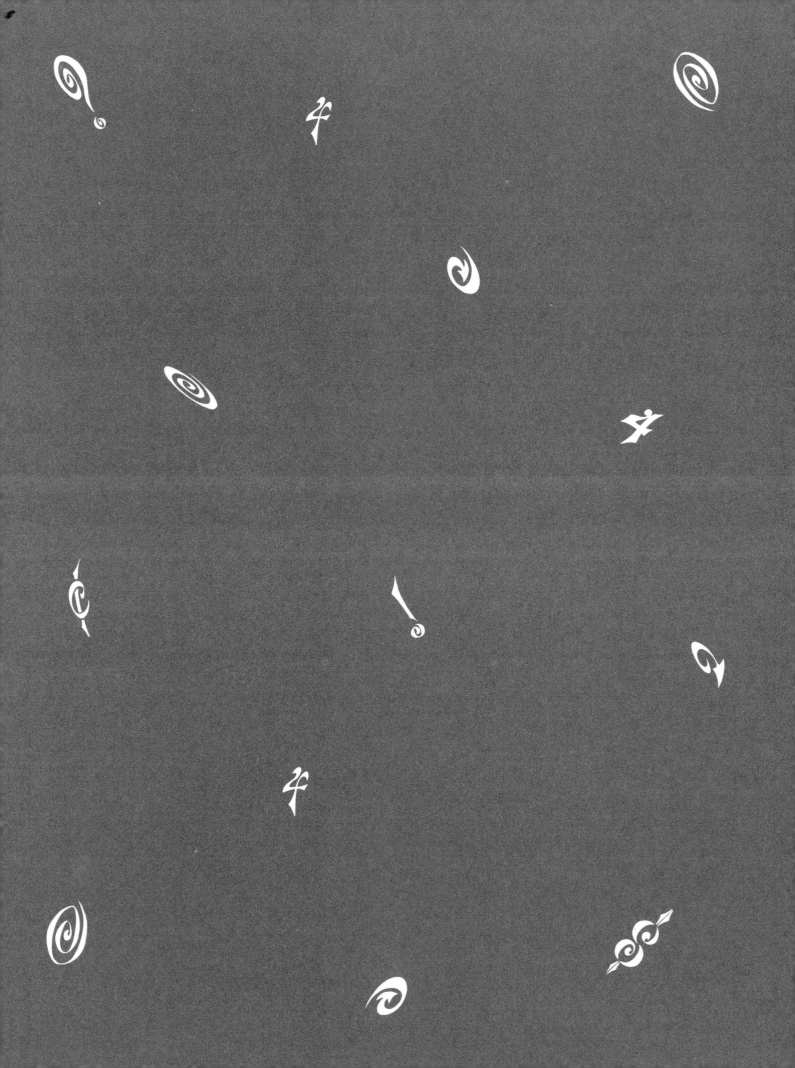